The Stone of Destiny

Alexandria Adair

RIVERSONG
BOOKS

An Imprint of Sulis International Press
Los Angeles | Dallas | London

THE STONE OF DESTINY

ISBN (print): 978-1-958139-61-5
ISBN (eBook): 978-1-958139-62-2

Published by Riversong Books
An Imprint of Sulis International
Los Angeles | Dallas | London

www.sulisinternational.com

Contents

O Flower of Scotland
When will we see your like again?
That fought and died for
Your wee bit hill and glen
And stood against him
Proud Edward's army
And sent him homeward
To think again.

The hills are bare now
The autumn leaves lie thick and still
Over land that is lost now
Which those so dearly held
And stood against him
Proud Edward's army
And sent him homeward
To think again.

Those days are passed now
And in the past they must remain
But we can still rise now
And become the nation again
That stood against him
Proud Edward's army
And sent him homeward
To think again.

—"Flower of Scotland", Scottish (unofficial) national
anthem, composed by Roy Williamson and the *Corries*

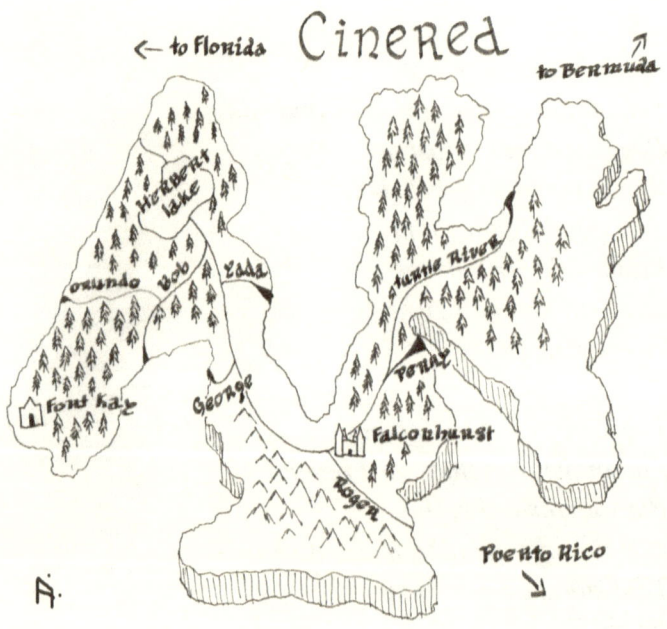

To all Jacobites: past, present, and future.

Acknowledgements

Thank you to all who helped me create my book.

DANIEL SCHWABAUER for his amazing "One Year Adventure Novel" curriculum

EVELYN ELLIOTT, social media aid

HARPER, my cousin, for the idea of Cinerea.

ELLA SILVER, and BRADEN OATES: my readers

KYLIE OATES: my editor

MY BROTHER for being a fellow Jacobite

MY MOM for reading the whole thing

1. I Become the Center of an Audacious Plot

As usual, I was having The Nightmare.

I was there: the place I hated most in the world. Physically, I had only been there once, but I saw it every night in my mind. With me was James, who had been my cousin and best friend. In fact, he was the only friend I'd ever had.

Just as on that horrible day two years ago, I stood with James on the cliff edge, gazing out towards the sea. It was a perfect sunny day, rare for this part of the country, with the cool sea breeze rising from the Atlantic Ocean.

Until our peace was shattered.

Looking behind me, something seemed strange about the rolling hills of the little port city of Oldshore, far in the north of Scotland. Something was there—an animal, maybe, walking along the side of one of the hills. I moved towards it.

"Where are you going?" asked James.

"Thought I saw something on that hill over there," I replied.

"I'm very glad our families decided to vacation here," James continued. "It's a beautiful place."

Those were the last words he ever said.

As I took another step towards the hill in my dream, I was thrown off my feet and a great boom shook the ground. Rolling into a rocky ditch, I covered my ears, but it was useless. They were already hurting. I scrambled to my feet, screaming out my cousin's name.

My head hurt so much I couldn't think straight, much less walk correctly. I stopped just in time. Right before me was the cliff-edge! Over ten feet of solid rock had been blown up by explosives—probably dynamite. And James was gone. I would never see him again.

*

My alarm went off, early as usual. I got up and dressed, and proceeded to gather my books and laptop to go to university. I packed everything in my briefcase and headed downstairs to find something to eat before I went. I was surprised to be confronted by three men at the bar drinking coffee.

I knew the two that were seated on the stools—my father and my cousin Jacob. The one whom I didn't know was standing and leaning on the counter. I had seen him once or twice, in conferences with my father, but never found out who he was. They were all staring at somebody's laptop, nodding and stroking their chins, until my father looked up and saw me. The other two also turned to stare at me. I shifted my weight awkwardly.

"We were just waiting for you, son," said my father. "Come take a look at this." He turned the laptop to face me. On the screen was a news video playing of a middle-aged man standing outside Edinburgh Castle in Scotland, reciting some kind of poem. The poem went like this:

In ancient, far off days of old
The Kings would sit upon a Stone
That Stone which was the Scottish throne
Far back in time, forgotten, cold.

The greatest Kings of Scotland seen
Living in a land of green
Prosperity did fill the land
Till Edward came with heavy hand.

Edward then the Stone did take
And people trembled as he spake
"Now I shall rule all your land
And all shall feel my iron hand."

Now Edward went to England
Did not withdraw his iron hand
He put the Stone on his own throne
That lay beneath his silver dome.

Many centuries now have passed
The Stone now lies in case of glass
To Scotland then it did return
That land of leaf and hill and fern.

Someday a new threat shall arise
Its head, a man consumed by lies
A boy will have a choice to make
And he must choose for Scotland's sake.

The boy has lost his only friend
The Stone to Cinerea he must send
The lost one will no more be lost
The boy will pay a heavy cost.

The boy must find a mighty sword
Worn by a mighty Scottish lord
The son of traitors shall be slain
By one who holds the traitor's bane.

The traitor was Sir John Mentieth
The owner of a mighty fief
Gave up Wallace to his death
He ever breathed the traitor's breath.

Scotland sometime shall rebel
If they will win now none can tell
If they do their King will be
The greatest King from sea to sea.

And on the Stone he must be crowned
Or this all cannot come around
Our King, O hasten to this land
And free us all from Edward's hand!

"Well?" All three men said, turning to me.

"Quite an interesting piece of historical lore," I said, and headed to the refrigerator to take out some eggs.

"Well, not all of it is history," said my cousin. "The first five stanzas are. I suppose you've heard of the Stone of Destiny?"

"Of course I have," I responded as I cracked eggs into a pan. "Don't you remember? I'm a history major."

"Mmm," hummed Jacob. "University. People seem to think it's the best thing on the planet."

Says the champion rugby player, I thought. Jacob had played rugby since he was a kid, but a devastating injury had prevented him from going professional. Since then, he had done absolutely nothing besides waste the family's money.

"Just to ensure you remember," said my father, "please remind us what the Stone of Destiny is?"

"Yes, it's an old relic that the Scottish people thought was magical," I replied, as I toasted some bread.

"That's some of it. However, you don't grasp the full meaning. The Scottish people believe that whoever is crowned on the Stone will rule Scotland. That is why Edward took it. But recently this madman—I forget his name—has been spouting this prophecy everywhere that claims Scotland is going to rebel."

"Rebel!" I exclaimed, turning from my fried eggs.

"Yes, rebel." This was the first time the strange man had spoken. His voice was subtle and low, and sent chills down my spine. "We must stop the rebellion. Do you not know that if the Scottish were to take back the lands they once possessed, your father, Lord Henry, would lose all of his estates? And so, subsequently, there would be nothing for you to inherit. To stop the rebellion, we need to stop the prophecy. To do that, we need to destroy the Stone of Destiny."

"Oh, don't do that!" I exclaimed. "Do you know how old that stone is? It's a piece of history! It's—"

"A chunk of rock?" prompted Jacob.

"Well, yes," I conceded, "but that doesn't make its historical value less. Let them keep it, I say. The exiled Stuart kings never had any heirs. It's just a nice story, and I think it'd be awfully cruel to destroy something that to them is so valuable."

"So you don't believe the old stories?" Asked my father.

"No, of course not. There's history and then there's myth. The stuff about the Stone of Destiny is just myth. Sure, their kings have been crowned on it for hundreds of years, but it doesn't give them supernatural power or anything. It's a royal symbol, just like the Crown Jewels are for us English."

"Did you ever take it into consideration that the Scottish people might not care whether the stories are true or not? Perhaps the Stone has supernatural power. Perhaps not. That doesn't matter. What matters is what the Scots think. If they think it has supernatural powers and are willing to fight to re-instate their nonexistent king, it doesn't matter whether the myths are true or if the man they put on the throne is really a Stuart. All that matters is whether they believe it enough."

I didn't know what to say, but I remembered my eggs, and flipped them onto the piece of toast.

"I repeat", said the strange man, "we need to destroy the Stone."

"Scots won't like that," I said.

"It doesn't matter what the Scotch like. They've been unhappy for centuries since we exiled their precious Stuarts, and we told them their Bonnie Prince Charlie died an alcoholic in France."

"Thought they voted to stay in the UK some years ago," I said, taking a bite of my egg sandwich.

The strange man gave a strange smile. "Between you and me, that was a brilliant piece of political manipulation. I'm sure you've read about that type of thing in your studies?"

"You mean..." I trailed off, "you rigged it? How dishonest!"

"It was best for them. They need protection from themselves. They don't know what's good for them. And, well, as for the honesty, when you get older, you'll learn that things that are wrong for ordinary people are not wrong for highly placed politicians like us. We control the world. Nobody will know about the—er —measures we had to take to secure their safety."

"Everybody's going to know when you steal the Stone and destroy it," I said.

"There are ways to explain it off. There can always be a fire, or maybe the Italian Mafia, or a convenient terrorist attack."

I was disgusted. I had had enough. I finished my sandwich in a big bite and picked up my briefcase.

"I've got to go," I said, my mouth full of sandwich. "Or I'll be late to class."

"One moment," replied my father. "When you were little you used to like the fairy stories about heroes and all. There is a Quest, and where there is a Quest, there must be a Hero. The Quest is to destroy the Stone of Destiny. The Hero is you."

"No, no, no," I said, "I don't want to be a hero anymore. I'm a university student. I haven't got time to spare. I really must be going. Exams are next week." I took a step to leave.

"I never gave you a choice," said my father. "The Quest can wait 'till your holiday. It won't take long. We need somebody who's not currently known to do this Quest. This patriotic expedition. This—"

"I need to go to class," I said.

"Just take this along with you," said Jacob, handing me an envelope. "Open it when you're alone. Sorry, I can't stay longer, Uncle Henry, I've got to go do something. See you tonight." Jacob turned and pulled a gold-brocaded coat off the hook, grabbed his hat off the stand, and walked out carrying a gold handled walking stick. I wondered why he had one—he certainly didn't need it. During daily life, his injury really didn't bother him. He was twenty-seven, and an amateur body builder, as far as his injury allowed. He was driven away by a chauffeur in a Rolls-Royce Phantom.

The university wasn't far, but the whole walk and the classes after it seemed like a blur after what I had just experienced. When I got home, my father and the stranger were still there—in the study, this time.

"Did you open the envelope?" my father asked.

"Not yet," I said.

"Open it," he replied.

I did so. Inside was a precisely folded letter stamped with the royal seal of England. I broke it and took a look at the first few lines:

Kenneth Phynndragon

Spy For His Royal Majesty the King Edward of England

I set the letter down, not wanting to read anymore. "This is addressed to someone else!" I said, dreading what I would hear next. "Kenneth Phynndragon is not my name!"

"It's your name now," my father informed me. "Don't worry, it's just temporary. We needed to change your identity a little for our mission. Go and finish reading the letter. We have some private business to discuss."

I opened it up fully and rolled my eyes as I saw a copy of the prophecy thingy in there. One verse of that poem had caught my attention—the ninth, because of the name in it—Sir John Mentieth.

"Father?" I asked. "What about the part that talks about Sir John Mentieth? Isn't that Jacob's father?"

"Quite coincidental," replied my father, getting up. "Really, you don't need to worry yourself much about the poem. It's gibberish anyway."

I went to my room and threw the letter down on my desk and stared out the window. *West.* My window faced west out over the sea. I couldn't stand the sea anymore. Not since James died. I wished the nightmares would stop. I wished he would come again. But I couldn't have that. James was dead.

I reached for the letter and scanned it again. There was a copy of that prophecy thing in there. My eyes locked on one verse.

The boy has lost his only friend
The Stone to Cinerea he must send
The lost one will no more be lost
The boy will pay a heavy cost.

2. I DISCOVER MY DESTINY FROM A COMPLETE STRANGER

Straightening my tie, I placed the *Do Not Disturb* door hanger on the door of my hotel room and hurried out down the stairs to the lobby. I walked anxiously down the hallway looking for Conference Room 22B, where I was to meet an experienced Edinburgh Museum curator who would teach me about my new job.

I opened the door and walked in. Two men were there, waiting for me. One must have been about sixty, with unkempt balding brown hair that reminded me of a coconut. The other was around forty, and by contrast had well combed dark brown hair and a navy blue two-piece suit like mine.

"Hello," I said, rather nervously. "I'm Kenneth Phynndragon, the new docent."

"Welcome, Mr. Phynndragon," said the man in the suit. "I'm Malcolm Stuart. And my colleague here is—"

"Chester Dunnigan," finished the other man. "Nice to meet you."

I sat down at the table, and Mr. Stuart turned to me.

"I'm sorry if ye expected somethin' more normal," he said in a thick Scottish accent, "but naething is normal around here anymore."

"Wait," I said in disbelief. "You're the man that was on TV reciting that weird poem!"

"Ye're correct," replied Mr. Stuart. "I've been on TV many times now. And it's because o' that poem that we want tae talk tae ye."

"Sorry," I said, "but I'm not interested in that poem. I'd like to know about my new job. Things like my duties, and hours, and stuff."

"Look, Mr. Phynndragon," said Mr. Dunnigan, "we didn't bring you here to talk about docent duties, or to hire you. It's something much more serious than that."

I didn't know how to respond, so I tried to remember what my father had told me to do.

We've got you a new ID and everything, and we've already sent an application for you at the Edinburgh Museum. Act normal and genuinely do your job until we notify you to let us in. You'll need to get us into the room where the Stone of Destiny is. Don't worry about getting out—we'll handle that. And when you're done, you'll be a huge hero, and you'll be all over the place famous. Just do it, okay?

"Alright," said Mr. Stuart, "let's back up a bit. So ye obviously know about the poem, an' ye've heard it too, right?"

"Right," I said, hesitantly.

"Well, basically this poem first goes over the history o' Scotland an' the Stone o' Destiny. How Edward took it, and its return many years later. These last six lines are prophetic, and the time is at hand for them tae come true. They come after the 'new threat' mentioned in verse six. Another enemy will come, and he will be consumed by lies. A boy,—" here he glanced at me, "will make a choice for Scotland. That boy has lost his only friend, and he'll take the Stone tae Cinerea. Then whoever the lost one is will be found, but the boy will pay a great price. But first he has tae kill his enemy, who is the traitor's son. The son of Sir John Mentieth."

"Who was Sir John Mentieth?" I asked. "My cousin's father has that name, but I thought it was a coincidence."

"Sir John Mentieth," said Mr. Dunnigan, "betrayed William Wallace in the late 1290s."

"Oh," I said, "so Sir John's son must be long dead by now."

"Depends on how ye look at it," said Mr. Stuart. "They could be meaning the literal son o' the man who betrayed William Wallace, or a male descendant, or simply a man whose father was named Sir John Mentieth! That's the way of prophecies: they never tell you very much and leave a lot to imagination."

"So what is the traitor's bane?"

"The sword o' William Wallace. It's at the Wallace monument in Stirling."

"Sometime after all that happens," continued Mr. Dunnigan, "the heir to the throne of Scotland will come, and if he is to be recognized as the real King, he must be crowned on the Stone of Destiny. If that is gone, the King won't be able to be crowned, and Scotland will continue to be subjugated and abused by the

English. However, if the King is crowned, he will be the greatest King that has ever been, and he will free Scotland from England's rule."

"So what does all this have to do with me?" I queried.

"Well, I'm sorry this had tae happen tae ye," said Mr. Stuart, "but we—I mean Mr. Dunnigan and I—think ye're the boy in the prophecy."

"That can't be true," I protested. "I'm no hero. I'm eighteen. I have no idea where Cinerea is, and why would I want to help Scotland out? I'm English. My family is English. I was born in England."

"Ye're sorely mistaken," laughed Mr. Stuart. "Did ye ken that yer mother is part Scottish?"

"Have you been spying on me?" I asked.

"Aye, we have. We've known aboot this prophecy for years, and ye've been appointed to help fulfill it."

"I'm sorry," I said, "But I just can't believe you. I just can't do it." I stood up to leave.

"Donnae go just yet," said Mr. Stuart. "Everythin' happens for a purpose, an' it's all part of the plan. The fact that ye're here, the happenings in yer past, every-thin' screams out that ye're the hero we're lookin' for. Donnae let us down."

"Okay," I said, returning to my seat. "I don't know what to say. I'm not a hero. I don't want to be a hero. I can't take a three-hundred pound rock to Cinerea, wherever and whatever that might be. I just can't do it. And I don't even understand why! What has England done to Scotland that you want to break away so bad? Why is England the bad guy?"

"What has England done tae Scotland?" Exploded Mr. Stuart. "Do ye no' read yer history, boy? All England has done is invade Scotland an' harry her for hundred's o' years, an' when we were finally under their heel, they banned our culture, bagpipes, the speakin' o' Gaelic, an' kilts."

"But that's not illegal anymore," I commented.

"We're also tired o' bein' ruled by a German king. If ye want tae know, he's not the true heir at all. The line of King Alfred went all the way tae Edmund Ironside, an' then he died, an' it went tae a cousin, then tae another cousin, an' then William the Conquerer took over. Edmund had a son though, and his son had a daughter, an' she married the Scottish King Malcolm Canmore. Then the line goes all the way down, until ye get tae the Stuart Kings. They were Catholic, and therefore unpopular. They got ousted for this German Protestant. I'm sure ye've heard of the rebellions of 1715 and '45. That was the true heir tryin' tae reclaim his throne. He couldna, and went into exile. However, there is an heir, the true King of Scotland, waiting tae return. An' then, we'll be free. However, King Edward of England has gotten wind o' this, an' is determined to keep Scotland under his heel forever. Tae do that, all he has tae do is destroy the Stone of Destiny. The Clans wilna rise unless their proven King is crowned on the Stone."

"You can't run away from who you are meant to be," said Mr. Dunnigan. "We've been waiting for you— Scotland has been waiting for you for hundreds of years. Are you really going to let us down?"

"Kenneth," said Mr. Stuart, "I believe if ye take this quest, it will fulfill yer greatest wish."

My greatest wish! I ignored him. The only thing I really wanted was James back. But I couldn't have that. James was dead. Not lost. Dead. He would never come back again. My senses started swimming, and I slid forward until my face rested on the table. I heard voices in my head, whispering;

You have lost your only friend
The Stone to Cinerea you must send
The lost one will no more be lost
You will pay a heavy cost.

3. I START A CIVIL WAR

The Nightmare. Again.

I was back on the sea-cliffs facing west, and James was there again, just like he was every time I had this dream. But this time he turned to me and said:

"You really need to do it."

"Do what?" I asked.

"Save it. The Stone, I mean. Don't you understand that you were made for a quest? Isn't that what we've been pretending all our lives? That we were heroes, saving the world? You were made for this mission."

"Don't be ridiculous," I said, but then the explosion came, and it was black all over again. And James was gone once more, never to return.

"Kenneth?" A voice drew me back to reality. "Kenneth? Are ye alright?"

I opened my eyes to find Mr. Stuart standing over me.

"I'm fine, I think," I said, my voice shaking. "I'm so confused."

"Well, don't be," said Mr. Dunnigan.

"Chester! That isna helpful!" Chided Mr. Stuart.

"Thanks for your help," I interjected, "But I'm not interested in any quest. I'm not made for it. I can't do that alone."

"I never said ye were goin' tae have tae do it alone," said Mr. Stuart.

"Who would help me on such a hopeless mission?" I asked, not expecting a reply.

"We will!" Came two voices from outside the room. In walked a girl in jeans and a sweater, who reminded me of Mr. Stuart. A boy about my age or a little older followed her, but they did not look much alike. He was tall and athletic, but had very dark hair and eyes. A small Scottish terrier followed them in, wagging his tail in delight.

"Meet my children," explained Mr. Stuart. "Donald and Elise."

"Nice tae meet ye," they both said together.

"A pleasure, I'm sure," I said absently. "But still, I don't want any quest."

"Sleep on it, then," said Donald.

I took his advice.

I got up in the morning after having that strange version of The Nightmare again. Half of me said: *Do it. Do it for James. Do it for your newfound homeland you've come to love.*

The other half said: *you're a kid. You can't do it. You know nothing about the world. What do you care about a prophetic King? Just give the Stone to them and be done with it.*

But the traitor's bane…

You think you could do any kind of damage with a sword that's almost as tall as you are? Forget about it.

But who's the traitor? It has to be Jacob.

Look, it's a coincidence. I'm sure there's a lot of John Mentieths out there.

I mean, maybe…

You mean to say 'positively'. Just do your job, okay?

Whose definition of my job?

Stop arguing! What Jacob told you to do.

But what if he's the traitor?

So far, Mr. Stuart had succeeded. Now I couldn't bring myself to hand over the Stone, but I couldn't commit to a journey that could earn me life imprisonment for treason if I failed. My phone rang faintly in the desk drawer. I ignored it.

It's got to be a call from Jacob, I thought. *And I don't want to hear anything from him.* They had given me that phone before I came here to Edinburgh, along with my fake birth certificate that designated me as Kenneth Phynndragon, eighteen years of age. I hated that phone because it and the birth certificate were now my only tie to the plot I now desperately wanted to get away from. It was also secure so that nobody could eavesdrop on it.

That got me thinking after I saw a light blink on it when I closed my desk drawer. It wasn't in the normal place for a light either. I picked it up and inspected it. Nothing happened.

"Hello?" I said experimentally. The light blinked again.

That's creepy, I thought. *Nobody can eavesdrop on the phone, but the phone can eavesdrop on me!*

Another realization hit me. I had had it with me when I was talking with Mr. Dunnigan and Mr. Stuart.

It overheard our entire conversation! Jacob knows everything now! I thought about throwing it out the window, but decided not to when I saw the crowded sidewalk down below.

What am I going to do? I asked myself. *How do I get out of this and be me again?* I turned and gazed out the window. *Why is the sidewalk so crowded? It's only seven in the morning.* After looking out longer and seeing nothing that gave me a clue, I decided to go down and see.

Flinging the phone down on the floor, I buttoned my coat and went down the stairs. I looked about nervously. The air was full of anxiety, with people talking in whispers and hurrying about. I knew something wasn't right, and I had an awful feeling that I was at fault.

Walking aimlessly about, I ran into Mr. Dunnigan. "What in the world is going on?" I asked.

"They've come for it," whispered Mr. Dunnigan. "And for you."

"What?"

"For the Stone," clarified Mr. Stuart, who had come up behind me.

"Who's come for it?"

"The English army."

I said nothing, but looked at the ground.

"What are ye goin' tae do about it?"

"Show me where it's kept," I said. *Wow,* my brain replied. *You just put your foot in it, and you can't take it out now.*

"Ye're takin' the quest then?"

"I am. Also, I need the sword."

Was I making a really horrible mistake? I supposed I would find out pretty soon.

I hurried off, following Mr. Stuart. We exited the hotel and ran down the street. Mr. Dunnigan had gone off to find Donald, Elise, and Mr. Stuart's van. I began to breathe hard, trying to keep up with Mr. Stuart

We slowed down as we approached the castle and showed our ID's. Hurrying past statues of Robert the Bruce and William Wallace, we climbed a steep paved road that led up to another gate. The guard recognized Mr. Stuart and let us though, but he warned us that trouble was afoot.

"Of course, heard all aboot it," said Mr. Stuart. "We need tae make sure nothin' crazy happens an' things donnae get vandalized."

We rushed past St. Margaret's Chapel and entered the Royal Palace. Taking several twists and turns, we hurried down the main way, around several displays, up some stairs, through a narrow corridor, up more stairs, and then finally arrived.

I hurried to move the rope barriers as Mr. Stuart made a beeline for the glass case in the center of the room and pulled out his key ring. From the opposite door, Donald and Elise entered with a large dolly. Donald ran forward to help his father with the Stone, and they began the slow work of shifting it onto the dolly.

"How much time do ye think we've got?" Asked Donald, struggling with the weight.

"Donnae know." Responded Elise. "Probably not enough." At that moment someone's cell phone dinged.

"That's mine," grunted Mr. Stuart. "It might be Beau or Hill." He freed up a hand to dig in his pocket and handed it to Elise.

"Not good," she informed us as she read the text message. "It's Hill. He says that Mentieth's on his way."

"How close is he?"

Elise was rapidly texting. Another ding.

"He's almost inside the castle."

4. I Help Steal a Three Hundred Pound Rock

I held the dolly as Mr. Stuart and Donald slid the Stone onto it. Elise pulled a large sheet from Donald's backpack and covered up the Stone. She threw open the door at the far side of the room, and we began to run.

Back in the main square, everything was mayhem. People were screaming and hiding at the sounds of gunfire. Keeping our heads low, we hurried back through the portcullis gate. The gateman was gone. Suddenly, Donald and Mr. Stuart swerved the cart into a narrow opening and Elise pushed me inside.

"What is it?" I started to ask, but Donald clapped a hand over my mouth and nodded to the entrance. Soldiers in camouflage marched past us, carrying the St. George flag.

"Right, left, right, left," someone was calling out. I recognized the voice. It was that of my cousin, Jacob.

After they passed, we hurried on down the steep road back to the esplanade. Two men met us at the gatehouse and took over for Mr. Stuart and Donald.

Mr. Dunnigan was at the wheel of a grey van, and he backed it into the esplanade. Mr. Stuart, Donald, and the two others began lifting it into the trunk.

Someone shouted behind us. Mr. Dunnigan jumped out of the driver's seat.

"I'll delay them!" He said. "Go on as soon as you can! I'll hold the fort."

We finally got the Stone up and slammed the trunk door. Soldiers with guns pointed at us ran up. Mr. Dunnigan stepped forward and began to speak.

"Get in!" Yelled Donald, pulling me into the third row of the van with him. The two other men jumped in the row in front of us, and Mr. Stuart drove with Elise and her Scottish terrier in the passenger seat. We roared away, but not before there was a gunshot. I twisted in my seat and saw Mr. Dunnigan lying on the pavement with blood all over the back of his head.

"They just killed him!" I screamed. "They killed Mr. Dunnigan!"

"Sorry, kid," said one of the men in front of me, with an obviously foreign accent. "A lot of people are going to die before this business is over. Probably us too."

"Why?" I asked. "Why are people going to die?"

"Don't you know? We've just started a civil war. The English army and the Scottish guard are fighting in the streets of Edinburgh. There's no turning back now."

"Beauregard's right," said Mr. Stuart. "We've really gotten ourselves mixed up in a crazy adventure."

"Who?" I asked.

"I'm Beauregard," said the man, "and this is my father, Hillel."

"Call us Beau and Hill," interjected Hillel.

Both men were strange-looking, wearing beanies that covered their ears. Long black hair protruded from underneath. They were very handsome, and I couldn't tell how old they were.

"Oh," I said. I was still confused and upset about Mr. Dunnigan. I was upset about everything. I couldn't believe that I had done what I just did. I was a criminal now.

"Why is this so important?" I demanded. "We just got Mr. Dunnigan killed—for a rock! And lots more people are going to die. Why is the Stone more important than them?"

"That's a hard question," said Mr. Stuart. "But it's a nation at stake. Our freedom an' the freedom o' our children. The Scottish people have been waitin' for the day when they can break away from England. We've been waiting for the day when the sixth, seventh, an' eighth verses o' the prophecy can be fulfilled—when the Stone goes tae Cinerea. We're waitin' for the King tae come. We're willin' tae fight for the Stone an' the King, if ye are."

We left the main city and began to enter the suburbs. We drove around a neighborhood, and then pulled into a driveway.

"Where are we?" I asked.

"This is our house," said Donald. "We're goin' tae stop here and get supplies."

"Supplies?" I said. "Where are we going?"

"Halfway across Scotland and over the Atlantic Ocean," replied Elise. "Tae the island o' Cinerea."

We drove into the garage and piled out. Elise, Beau, and Mr. Stuart ran inside to gather supplies. Donald and Hill began pulling stuff off of shelves and putting it into bags. They tossed them to me, and I loaded them into the trunk.

"What is all this?" I asked.

"A lot o' food" replied Donald, "also lots o' petrol. We donnae ken when we're goin' tae be able tae fill up our tanks."

When we got into the car, Beau asked Elise to pull out the road maps. Mr. Stuart objected, saying that he knew the way to Inverness. Beau leaned forward and began to speak, but it was so quiet that I couldn't hear, since I was in the third row. I could see parts of Mr. Stuart's face in the rearview mirror, and I could tell that he wasn't happy.

I leaned over and whispered to Donald, "Has something gone wrong?"

"Donnae ken, I canna hear them," replied Donald, "But maybe it's because Beau wasna able tae get the sword. Maybe we'll be headin' that way now."

"Sword? You mean Wallace's?"

"Aye. Looks like we're goin' to have another narrow escape."

*

So we had to sneak in yet another museum. This time it was the National Wallace Monument in Stirling, and I wasn't allowed to go in. Not that I minded. According to Beau this mission "needed stealth and professionalism, and even with that, it still might fail." I had to stay in the car with Donald and Elise. Donald drove the car around the block, trying not to look suspicious, then parked in an empty parking spot next to a blue estate car.

"Any idea what the plan is?" I asked him.

"Nae. I highly doubt they have any plan themselves." He opened the door and stepped out of the car, watching the entrance. "Everything's mayhem. It shouldna be too hard tae go inside an' get it. It's getting out that's the problem."

That wasn't very encouraging. I was hoping to hear some intricate scheme that would involve us getting the sword and all escaping safely. I started regretting my spur-of-the-moment decision to steal a Stone and a sword and lead a rebellion.

Shouting disturbed my musings as the car door slammed as Mr. Stuart got in, changing places with Donald. Beau and Hill piled into the middle and handed me a long, heavy object wrapped in a piece of fabric. It was quite a job, considering that its length was above five feet. I unwrapped it, wondering if I was really worthy to be using the sword of such a legendary hero.

"You do realize," I said to nobody in particular, "that this sword is as long as me?"

"Not quite," Elise commented, always the one for accuracy.

"Ye'll get used tae it," Donald reassured me.

I found that hard to believe. "Are you sure?"

"If ye're the hero we hope ye are, aye."

I was sure that I wasn't. This sword was forged for a Scotsman over six feet tall and likely very muscular, unlike my five—foot eight self. I had never played sports, and spent most of my time reading or studying. Plus I rarely would go outside if I could avoid it after the incident with James. Being outside frightened me, and it still did. I hadn't felt comfortable since I left home.

*

When we had driven through the countryside for an hour or two through heavy traffic, Mr. Stuart pulled over so that Beau and Donald could fill up the car with some of the petrol we had brought along with us.

"While we're stopped," he said to me, "let's see what ye can do with a sword."

"Not much, I'm afraid," I replied. "Back at home my father made me take some fencing lessons, but they're nothing like using this." It was quite a job to lift it, much less swing it.

Mr. Stuart unsheathed his own sword, a basket hilted broadsword about three and a half feet long. It looked like something from the 1700s. I began to wish that William Wallace had either been a dwarf or had lived in the eighteenth century instead of the eleventh.

"No, no, NO! Don't hold it like that! Ye donnae want tae kill anyone on yer first day of trainin'!"

"No sir," I sighed.

"Okay, yes, there ye go! Alright now, swing at me. Not too wild now!"

I grunted with the strain as I raised up the sword and swung it clumsily at Mr. Stuart. He met me with a jarring blow that made my hands ring. I dropped the sword. Mr. Stuart cried out in frustration.

"That's the last thing ye want to do in a duel," he scolded. "How do ye expect to defeat an enemy when ye cannae even hold up yer own sword?"

I held my tongue, resisting the urge to complain. That would get me nowhere. Before I could try again, Donald called from the car, announcing that everything was ready. Mr. Stuart stomped off back to the driver's seat and left me. Scottie (Elise's Scottish terrier) followed him, ignoring me. I picked up my sword and sheathed it, then kicked a tuft of grass.

"That's what I think of swords," I muttered with disgust.

This time Elise sat in the middle row with Beau as Mr. Stuart and Hill debated in the front seat in hushed tones. They must have gotten upset because their voices grew louder.

"Really? After all that work—"

"I'm sorry, Malcolm, it isn't our fault…"

"I know it isnae, Hill, but ye understand our situation, right?"

"Of course I do! You know what we have to lose, and Kenneth most of all."

"I still cannae help being frustrated though…is there any way we could get a different ship?"

"Malcolm, it's impossible unless I got one from Cinerea. There's a lock on all the ports—no ships can come in or go out."

"That isnae a problem. Getting the ship is the problem."

"I'll ask Elise to see about arrangements. We might be able to get there by chopper."

"All right, Hill! See tae it! I hope it works out."

5. The Filling Station Explodes

We drove for hours, only stopping occasionally to pull out petrol cans from our ever-dwindling supply. Donald slumped in the seat next to me, probably napping. I wished that I had brought a book—a good long one. Our next stop, Donald and Elise switched seats.

"I wanted tae show ye somethin'," said Elise, opening a large three-ring binder. There were lots of plastic slip sheets with old documents inside.

"Old maps!" I said, flipping the pages.

"Thought ye'd be interested, bein' a history major and all," she said.

I continued to look and study the maps. Many were of Scotland. Some were historical documents—letters and such, letters that I had never seen. Then I flipped the page to reveal a marriage license. I tried to decipher the names written.

"It's Prince Charlie's marriage license," said Elise. "He really was married, you know. It's a whole conspiracy invented by the English. They said that he didna marry her, but he did. He had tae hide the license, and hide the child. If they found out that he was legitimate, he would hae been killed."

There was a pause as I continued to flip the pages.

"It really is too bad," Elise started to say.

"What's too bad?"

"That ye had tae leave it—university and all. To save a country that is nothing to ye."

"Well, I suppose I was (and maybe still am) rather reluctant. I think I'm starting to change my mind. Since I'm a history major, it's sort of my job to save history."

"What made ye change yer mind?"

"Well, my ambition was to learn about history and teach it someday, sitting in a stuffy classroom grading badly written papers...but this is different. I'm saving history (or at least trying to.) I get to make history. I might be remembered in history. Even if I fail, people will remember I tried. People will remember all of us as people who gave everything they had for the cause. Even if we fail, our stories might inspire the next generation to take up arms for the true King. Becoming a legend is a whole lot better than becoming a professor."

"Nice speech," grumbled Beau. "All well and good for people who've got a silly thing called hope. Try to be realistic, kid. If we fail this, there's going to be nobody left to write stories about us. And even if there were, they wouldn't be allowed to print them. Nope. This is it. If we mess this up, there's no way the real King will have a chance."

"Beau," said Hill, "has been listening to far too much radio. We all got sick of it so he's got it in earbuds now. This is what it's like."

He turned the radio volume up.

...Edinburgh being shelled by heavy artillery... Dundee and Glasgow are half destroyed...Trillions of pounds in damage expected...we don't know how the country will survive after this...

"That's enough for today," said Mr. Stuart, switching the radio off. "How about somethin' more pleasant? I spy with my little eye somethin'....green!"

"It's Scotland," groaned Donald. "*Everythin'* is green."

*

Pulling onto the side of the empty highway, we piled out of the auto and dragged out five more two-gallon gas cans from the trunk. Beau was searching through bins and bags, and Donald was digging through the roof rack.

"Is everything okay?" I asked.

"Of course not," griped Beau. "Nothing's ever okay anymore."

"Though the main problem right now," added Hill, "Is that those five cans are all the gasoline we've got left."

"All the what?"

"Gasoline. You silly English call it petrol."

Shoving all the bags and bins back in the trunk, we slammed the door and loaded ourselves back in. Elise was rifling through the glove box and pulling out maps.

"There's a filling station about twenty miles from here," she said. "Think we can risk it?"

"We've got nae choice," said Mr. Stuart, starting the engine again. "We'll either have tae fill up or leave the car. We've a long way tae go still."

"Where exactly are we headed again?" I asked. "I thought I was supposed to be the hero here, and I have almost no idea where we are going and what we are doing."

"Okay," said Hill, "I'll give you a little bit of background. So the Stone of Destiny is an ancient relic that the Kings of Scotland have been crowned on for thousands of years. They say that the true kings must be crowned on the Stone, and in the late 1200s, it was stolen by Edward, as you now know. In the late 1990s, it got returned to Edinburgh Castle. And now we've stolen it because we've got to take it to the Island of Cinerea for safekeeping, and to fulfill the prophecy."

"We haven't told you this yet, but Beau and I live on Cinerea. Cinerea is the last piece of the old world—the magical world, you might say. We're the reason that so many ships and planes are lost over the Bermuda Triangle. The Fence keeps out unwelcome visitors, and if they come too close, they are destroyed. That's where we're bound."

"What is our plan for getting there?" I asked.

"We are nae sure yet!" Yelled Mr. Stuart from the driver's seat.

"We aren't?" Said Beau in surprise. "I thought Elise made arrangements."

"It's rather complicated," said Elise. "Herbert and his gang can carry a person, but they canna take the Stone. It'll have tae continue on by car tae the coast. We were nae able tae hire any boats on this side of the Atlantic, so Beau, Hill, and I will go to Cinerea via Herbert and bring back a ship, and hopefully ye'll all be there when we get back."

"Any idea how long that's goin' tae take?" Asked Donald.

"Absolutely none," returned Elise. "Just make sure that ye're there when we come back."

"And where exactly is there?" I inquired.

"Oldshore."

"Oldshore!" Exclaimed Donald. "Why did ye have to choose the furthest place from here?"

Oh, no, I thought. *No! Not Oldshore! That's where The Nightmare happened!*

"That's what Percy, Mentieth, and the English will least expect," said Hill. "They will probably think it most likely that we will try to go to Oban or another city closer to here."

"Fat chance," grumbled Beau.

"Who are Percy and Mentieth?" I asked. I wondered if they meant my father and Jacob.

"The ringleader of the ones who want to destroy the Stone—"

"Hey!" Shouted Mr. Stuart suddenly. "Do ye see that?"

"See what?" I asked, craning my neck to see out the windshield.

"The water's glowin'!"

"That means time for us tae go," said Elise, grabbing her bags off the floor of the car. Mr. Stuart pulled the car off to the side and Beau, Hill, and Elise got out.

"Bye, Father and Donald!" Said Elise. "Make sure ye're there when we come back!"

"See ya!" said Hill.

"Not much chance of that," grumbled Beau as he slung an army backpack over his shoulder.

Mr. Stuart got out of the car, and talked to Elise for a few minutes. They embraced, then Elise hurried after Beau and Hill as Mr. Stuart returned.

We watched them disappear in silence, and Scottie stayed with Donald. Strangely enough, because he usually followed Elise wherever she went, but for some reason, Elise had explained, he was terrified of both heights and the ocean. Donald then took his turn driving, and I sat alone in the back seat with Scottie.

When we pulled into the filling station, Mr. Stuart got out and began filling us up. At that moment several things happened. The door of the mini mart opened, revealing several well-armed men heading straight for us. A car door slammed and several more came from behind the hedge. We were surrounded.

Mr. Stuart yanked the hose out of the car, and slashed it with his sword, spilling petrol out by the gallons. The men pulled out hand guns. They carefully avoided the slippery mess.

"Donald! Get out of here!" Yelled Mr. Stuart.

Two men were banging on the trunk, trying to open it. Donald began to open the door, but Mr. Stuart kicked it shut. "Get out!" He yelled again. "Remember the Stone and the King to come!"

The men opened fire as Donald stomped on the gas, and we roared off, leaving Mr. Stuart fighting alone. We ducked as bullets whizzed through the window. Donald's hands were white and shaking as he grasped the wheel.

"Are you okay?" I asked him, worried that he had gotten hurt. He looked away from me and grabbed his jacket from the console and put it on.

Scottie came and sat next to me as I stared out the window. I heard the voices in my head again, but they said something different now.

You're alone, they said.

I know that, I replied, inside my head. *Just give me my old life back. That's what I want.*

Really? Is it?

I guess not. What I really want is James back. I can't really go back to my old life without him.

Well, too bad. You're alone, they said, laughing.

Alone

You're alone

The lost one will no more be lost

The boy will pay a heavy cost.

You will pay a heavy cost.

6. I Utterly Fail

I looked back again to try and see if I could find Mr. Stuart, but we were too far away. I closed my eyes when I saw the flash, and then we heard an explosion. The gas station was now a smoking wreck.

"Donald!" I yelled. "Did you see that?"

"Sort of," he replied quietly, "but donnae get yer hopes up. Naebody could hae survived that."

Then it was done. Mr. Stuart was dead. I buried my head in my knees and cried.

*

Sometime later, I saw that Donald was slumping in the chair, and appeared to be fighting sleep.

"Donald," I offered, "you should let me drive. I'm not great, but I think you should take a break." Donald didn't reply but appeared relieved. He pulled the car over and stumbled to the passenger seat and promptly fell asleep. I looked at the gas tank. We were almost out. I hoped the traffic would be over soon—I hated driving in it, and it was worse since I was not the best driver.

I was in low spirits. Mr. Stuart's death was shocking, and Donald was no comfort. Our sad mood must have rubbed off on Scottie because all he did was sleep. We kept driving and driving and driving. The once beautiful countryside now was monotonous and boring as we kept going on. It got dark, and we still kept driving.

I pulled over and turned on the car light so that I could check the map. I looked over at Donald to see if he could help me, but he was still asleep. He had leaned the seat most of the way back and turned his face away from me. I reached over and shook him, telling him to wake up. When he didn't respond, I looked more closely at him. That was when I saw it. His jacket on the shoulder and chest was a funny color in some spots. I touched it, and it was wet.

In that moment, I began to panic. All this time I had had at least one person to help me get through it all, but now I was alone, and my friend was bleeding to death. I ran around the car, opened the passenger door and peeled his jacket and shirt off to check the wound. I could tell from one look that the little first aid kit in the glove box was not going to be very helpful. I grabbed a thin blanket from the back seat and began ripping it into strips, hoping I wasn't too late.

The wound was a small one, below his left shoulder. Donald had probably thought it was only a graze, and didn't really check on it. It made me feel worse thinking that he had probably ignored it because he hadn't wanted to scare me. The bullet was still in his body, and I didn't want to risk taking it out. I had to hope that he could survive long enough for me to get him some proper treatment.

I staunched the bleeding with his jacket, then attempted to clean the wound with the tiny can of Bactine spray that we had in the car. I used all of it. Then I padded the wound with the blanket strips and wrapped it up. It wasn't an easy job. Afterwards I grabbed Donald's water bottle and tried to get him to drink something, but he was completely limp and unconscious.

I had to think, and do it fast. It seemed that my best hope would be to keep on to Oldshore, and hope that Elise, Beau, and Hill would be back, or would come in time to help. So I climbed back in the driver's seat and kept going.

*

I squinted in the early morning sunlight. A sign said 'Oldshore: 10 km.' I looked down at the gas gauge. There might just be enough. Ahead of me another sign said 'Oldshore Checkpoint 1 km.' *Great. Just what I need.* I pulled onto the side of the road and covered Donald up with a blanket so that a guard might think he was only asleep. I returned to my seat and kept on.

*

Oldshore was a bustling little port town perched on the edge of a cliff. *Why, oh, why oh, WHY did it have to be on a cliff? I hate cliffs!* The road ran right next to a cliff too, with no guard rail. I tried not to look that way, afraid of becoming dizzy.

As we neared to the gate, the guard waved me to a stop. I rolled down the window and he peered in. I looked straight at him, and I recognized him. He was no guard, but had his hair neatly combed and wore a gold brocaded suit. He tapped on the door with a gold handled walking stick.

"Hello, Walter! Nice to see you again!" He sneered.

Walter. That's my real name.

"I know what you're up to," continued Jacob. Yes, it was Jacob. He had caught up to us.

Jacob laughed. "You're trying to save that little rock. A rock! That's all it is, Walter Percy! Tell you what. You give me the Stone; I give you your life back. What do you say? That's what you want, isn't it?"

I still didn't reply. No matter how much I wished for my old life, it wasn't what I wanted most. Nobody could give me James back. I hesitated. Six shadowy shapes began creeping out of the bushes on the side of the road. They slunk to the car and gathered around the trunk.

"Get the rock," Jacob ordered his men, "but leave the boy to me." In one swift movement, Jacob reached into the car from the window, unlocked my door, and opened it. He dragged me out, and I tried to fight back, but it was too late.

"What should we do with this one, Boss?" asked one of Jacob's men, pointing to Donald. "He looks asleep or dead."

Jacob turned to me. "Which is he?"

"Asleep," I answered. It was sort of the truth.

Jacob threw me on the ground right on the edge of the precipice—yes, it had been in this town on these very same cliffs that James had fallen off of two years before. Jacob was not gentle. He leaned a lot of weight on my chest, making it hard to breathe. The hilt of Wallace's sword dug into my back. I looked down, which was a mistake. The waters churned around sharp rocks that began to almost look like shark fins. I heard the scream, and I thought I felt the cliff shake.

"What's the matter?" Scoffed Jacob. "You scared of heights?"

I didn't reply. I was too frightened to move. Then Jacob grabbed my shoulder, rolling me halfway off the edge. Some loose pieces fell down the steep slope. "Ha!" Jacob snickered. "You have really failed this time. Remember it for the rest of your short life. Remember, Walter Percy." He pushed me away from him, over the cliff edge to the sea below.

Recovering my senses, I grabbed at the edge of the wall to slow my fall. Below me loomed the churning sea, and in the midst of it, I glimpsed a faint glittery multicolored glow. However, I didn't have time to ponder that, and I still grabbed at the cliff wall. I hoped to somehow grab onto a rock, but it all came falling off with me.

My hands and arms were torn and bleeding, but in my present predicament, I didn't feel them. The sea was getting closer and closer. That glow was still there, bigger and brighter. I shut my eyes and waited for the impact.

I hit the water so hard that I lost consciousness for a little while. When I woke up I was lying face down on something solid, but it was moving.

"What's happening?" I yelled.

"You just got rescued," replied someone from somewhere. I looked all around me, but I didn't see anything that might be talking to me. Then I looked down, and saw that I was lying on what that looked like a turtle shell, but every shape on it was a different rainbow color. It looked like it had been coated in glitter glue, and it glowed all over the place.

To the sides there were two flippers, with each scale a different sparkly color like the shell. I saw a head and a tail, and it struck me that it looked rather like a turtle, except for the glittery part.

I looked down. "Turtles don't talk," I said, hoping I hadn't gone insane. "That was just your imagination. Don't listen to it."

"Uh, hello!" The voice said again. "I think you're a little off track. Most turtles don't talk, but ones like me do."

"And what kind of turtle are you?" I ventured.

"A magic one, obviously! The name's Herbert. Sorry I can't shake your hand or anything, but I kinda need my flippers for swimming."

"Okay," I said, still trying to process. "So you're a magic turtle named Herbert. Got that. Now can you explain why you're here and what you are going to do with me?" I had made up my mind that this turtle wasn't evil, but I didn't really know whose side he was on.

"I'm from Cinerea," replied Herbert. "I'm to drop you off in this town called Durness. Hill sent me to find you."

"Okay, I guess," I replied. It would be a relief to see Hill again. It sounded nearly too good to be true. Then I remembered something.

"Herbert!" I cried. "What happened to Donald?"

"What about him?" Asked Herbert. "Was he with you?"

"He was, and he got a bad bullet wound just before we were captured. He was unconscious when I left him."

"That's too bad," responded Herbert. "I haven't heard anything about him. After I drop you off I'll try and collect some news. I've met Donald a few times. Nice guy. Hope he's okay."

After a little while, I could see the town of Durness not far away. Hill was supposed to be waiting there for me. Herbert left me at the edge of the pier, saying that though he could, he didn't want to go on shore and cause a scene.

"That's hardly what you need right now," he said. "Anyway, gimme a call if you need me!"

"I certainly will," I replied. "See you later."

I hauled myself out of the water and walked, dripping, back along the pier into the town. It was probably around sixty degrees and cloudy, and all I wanted was to get inside where it was warm. I looked around me, surveying the sidewalks and streets.

Where was Hill?

7. I GET LOST

I didn't see Hill anywhere, and I began to get nervous. *Herbert told me Hill was here. Hill told Herbert that he was here.*

Then a thought came to me.

Could Herbert have misheard?

That got me thinking.

So if Hill isn't here and Herbert took me to the wrong place, that means that Hill can be anywhere on this side of Hadrian's Wall. Or farther, maybe. So where is the place I'm supposed to be?

After that, a whole bunch of extremely comforting thoughts entered my head.

I'm probably going to die from exposure.

I'm going to run into Jacob.

Is Donald okay?

Those voices are going to bother me again.

Hill might think I'm dead.

What if Hill is dead? And Donald too!

What if Herbert's a traitor and isn't really not from Cinerea?

This last thought made me even more depressed than I already was. I liked the magic turtle a lot, and would be very disappointed if he turned out to be a traitor.

All of a sudden, I realized I was probably very conspicuous. I stood in the middle of the sidewalk, dripping wet, my arms and face scraped up and bleeding, staring into space, with a giant sword strapped to my back. I looked about me and made for a bench set in the sidewalk. As I got closer, I noticed a man that was walking around and tacking things up on the telephone poles.

"Hi there," I asked, trying to sound casual. "What are you doing?"

"Putting up these wanted posters," he said.

"Wanted posters?"

He ripped one off the pole next to us. "Yes." He handed it to me, and looked at me closer. "Aren't you a little wet?"

"Actually, yes, I am," I admitted, trying to laugh nonchalantly. "Tripped on the pier and fell in the water! But anyway," I trailed off, flattening out the paper, so I could read it. It read as follows:

Wanted: Dead Or Alive For High Treason
Against The King Of England.

Walter Percy, may be going as Kenneth Phynndragon, eighteen years old. Brown hair and green eyes. About 5'7".

Malcolm Stuart, age forty. Dark brown hair and blue eyes. 5' 11". Former Edinburgh museum curator.

Donald Stuart, age sixteen. Black hair and brown eyes. 6' 0"

Elise Stuart, age seventeen. Dark brown hair and blue eyes. 5'3"

Two men using the names Beauregard and Hillel. Tall, have black hair, and have American accents. Appear to be in their late twenties.

Large reward offered for the live capture or sufficient proof of the death of any of these people. Please bring any information to the local Constable.

Signed,

JACOB MENTIETH.

My heart nearly stopped. They knew my name and my alias…

"Hey," the man said suddenly. "What's your name?"

The question caught me off guard. "Ken—no, Walt—um, John. John Smith."

"Know those people in the picture?"

"No," I said. I looked down at the paper. There was my senior picture from high school, and one of the Stuarts with Scottie. The man continued talking.

"You're going to come with me, Mr. Smith."

"No, I'm not," I replied nervously. I reached up and grabbed the buckle of my back sheath, ready to undo it in case I had to use the sword. The man, however, was not going to allow me to do that. Before I had time to draw the sword, he had grabbed me and shoved me into the back of his car.

"You have no right to do this!" I protested as he began to handcuff me.

"Oh yes, I do," he replied, pulling an ID card out of his pocket. "Ed Keith of His Royal Highness's Secret Police at your service."

I was determined not to give up so easily. I couldn't get at my sword, but I swung my handcuffed fists at his face. Ed Keith grabbed me easily and shoved me back into the car. "I've had enough of you for today," he said angrily, aiming a punch at my face. That's all I remembered before everything went black.

I woke up on a hard bed in a holding cell. My head was spinning. I tried to stand up, but fell back down again. As I gradually became more aware of my surroundings, I overheard a conversation.

"Constable," a Voice said, "I've got news of some of the men on those wanted posters. Malcolm Stuart has been captured and is currently in a holding cell in Melness under charges of arson."

"Very good!" Replied the Constable. "I'll inform Mr. Mentieth at once!"

"That's not all," replied Voice. "Donald Stuart has also been captured and is also being held in Melness, facing charges of burglary of museum artifacts."

The constable was on the phone. "Hello? Is this Mentieth? Very good! Two of the men that you wanted are incarcerated in Melness. Another is held here."

Mr. Stuart alive? And Donald too! That was great news, even though we were all in a nasty predicament. I threw myself back on the bed and tried to think.

*

That night, I had The Nightmare again.

Back at the sea-cliffs, I stood with James on the edge. He turned to me and said:

"Don't lose hope! You can still be a hero!"

"No, I can't!" I said. "They've taken the Stone, and Mr. Stuart, and Donald, and William Wallace's sword. I'm a complete failure."

That's when the explosion came, for real this time.

I woke with a jolt and found part of my dream had come true! The hair on my face and hands was singed, and my skin hurt all over. The heavy doors to my cell had been damaged, and with one hard kick to the hinges I finished it off.

I dashed out of the cell and examined the wreckage. I hoped William Wallace's sword was still there. I tried to think about where they might put a sword, but couldn't, so I simply dug through the debris. I eventually found it, untouched, under the remains of a blackened desk. I buckled on the belt, and then shoved the sword in. It was tough to lift it so high. Then a figure came running to me out of the wreckage. It was Hill.

"Kenneth! Let's get out!" He said. Artillery shells began raining down on us. Planes flew overhead, some strafing the ground. People were running and screaming and, in general, causing so much mayhem, nobody really noticed us. We looked for the cover of buildings and tried to stay in the shadows. Once we were out of the city, we found ourselves alone in a wild country in cold weather with nothing but the clothes we had on and a few weapons. Hill had a fancy sword, a Taser, and a small handgun.

"How'd you find me?" I asked, finally.

"Herbert and Orlando." he replied.

"Who's Orlando?"

"Sorry, Kenneth! I forgot to mention that Herbert's got a whole gang of magic turtles at his call. Whenever one of us Cinereans goes out into the world, one of the turtles goes with us. When I didn't see you, I simply looked for one of Herbert's gang, and Orlando was patrolling the vicinity. He found Herbert, who had accidentally taken you to Durness instead of Melness."

"Have we got any plan?" I asked. "Should we try to rescue Mr. Stuart and Donald?"

Hill nodded. "That's pretty much our only hope now. We might also find the Stone in Melness."

However, that was a whole lot easier said than done. Melness was about thirty miles away by car across an inlet of the sea. We were going to need a boat.

*

I didn't want to have to do it, but I had to. We picked the oldest and least valuable rowboat from the dock and slipped it silently in the water. I felt really guilty stealing a boat like this, but the best thing we could do was to leave it on the other side and hope the owners would find it.

We rowed our way across Loch Eriboll and left the boat sitting openly on the edge, for its owner to maybe find. We threw the oars in and went on our way—the way to certain capture.

8. I FAIL AT SWORDPLAY

Hill and I stood with our backs to the prison wall, debating over which plan was more hopeless. Neither of us knew very much about breaking into prisons. I thought we should break in through a window, but Hill objected, saying that we could just run in the doors and try to startle them. I held on to my window idea until Hill told me that the windows had bars, and anyway they were probably highly monitored by security cameras. Then I brought up the same thing about the doors, so we abandoned that idea too. We slumped against the wall and waited for inspiration.

The light grew, and our danger with it. We wanted to get out into some better cover, but we didn't think we could without risking being picked up by the cameras. We didn't really even know if we were safe from cameras where we were. Our fears were reaffirmed by the sight of several neon signs saying *Smile, you're on camera*. There was one right in front of me and I stared at the yellow smiley face that seemed to be mocking me.

The prison door banged open and boots stomped along the path. I tried to quiet my breathing, but all it did was almost make me choke. Bullets whizzed over my head and shot wide of the face.

"You missed!" Someone said. "Lemme show you how to do it."

Instantly, five or six bullets buried themselves in the sign and completely obliterated the face.

"C'mon, Dan, let's get some food," said another man. "Phew! I'm glad my watch is done!"

"I'm with you, Dave," agreed Dan. "Get food, then sleep, and then our watch again." He shook his gun. "And pick up some ammo too. I'm low."

"You know those two new guys that we got?" Asked Dave.

"Yep. What about 'em?"

"I hear that they're gettin' picked up pretty soon. Some rich guy wants 'em—Jacob Mentieth's the name."

My ears perked up. We might stand a better chance of rescuing Mr. Stuart and Donald if they were outside the prison.

"Oh, him," said Dan. "The guy with the weird prophecy about him?"

"Didn't it say that he was the traitor's son or something, and that he's gonna get killed by Wallace's sword?"

"So it goes," laughed Dan. "Don't believe it, though. Those things never happen."

Their footsteps grew louder as they rounded the bend and headed our way. Hill looked at me and tapped the pommel of his sword. I understood the gesture and undid the back sheath of my sword. Jumping out of hiding, we swung the hilts of our swords and gave each of the guards a hefty blow with the pommel. Both were knocked out cold and collapsed on the ground.

I turned and looked straight into the lens of a security camera. I was so startled that I couldn't move or speak until Hill grabbed me and began pulling me away. We dashed down the street and down a dark alley, smack into Beauregard.

I yelped, not knowing who it was, until Hill clapped a hand over my mouth and whispered, "Beau! How'd you get here?"

"I came from Cinerea via Roger Red," answered Beau. "Still stiff from the trip. Whew! Crossing the Atlantic in twenty-four hours really chills you right through. But we haven't got time to talk." He gave a low whistle, and about thirty black-haired men similar to Beau emerged from the shadows. With them was Scottie, the little terrier I had thought dead. He ran up to me and I knelt down and started petting him.

"Are you all going to help us rescue Mr. Stuart and Donald?" I asked.

"Why else would we show up here?" Asked Beau. "At least, we're going to try. It's not likely we're going to accomplish anything else besides get ourselves killed."

*

I peered around the corner of the building, watching the police car approach.

"Tell us when," said Beau in a barely audible whisper.

I watched Mr. Stuart and Donald led out in handcuffs, two guards to each. I looked to the thirty-two men behind me, their Tasers ready. I pulled out my own. "Now."

Leaping out of hiding with a yell, we beset the eight or ten guards. I grabbed the arm of one and punched him in the face, but then he did the same to me and I fell over, letting go of him. I was never a good fighter.

I jumped up off the ground, and saw that Beau's men were already on the guards. I suddenly realized with a horrible start that we were right in the view of about three cameras, and that we were going to have to get out fast if we hoped to not be captured.

Someone started yelling "Do whatever you have to do! Kill them if you have to! Just stop them!"

I realized two awful things at once. Thing number one: that voice was coming from directly behind me. Thing number two: that voice belonged to my cousin, Jacob Mentieth.

I whirled around and fumbled for my back sheath so I could pull out the sword. It was a slow business, and Jacob laughed.

"So! You have gotten bolder, haven't you? Got a little army, too?"

A million ideas went through my head at once. However, the words that came out were:

"You're nothing but a coward!"

I stopped, realizing what I had just said. *Oh no,* I thought. *I've really gotten myself in trouble this time.*

"Oh, am I!" Said Jacob, coolly, not in the least angered by my words. "Really, Walter, I thought that you would be capable of something more eloquent than that. Do you think I am a coward? Look at yourself! Because of you, one of your friends is dead and two are captured, and the precious Stone that you were all trying to save is in my hands! If I am a coward, Walter Percy, then it is cowards who will always win the day."

"That's what you think," I maintained obstinately.

"Of course it's what I think. Actually, I more than think it. I know it." He looked with contempt at my sword. "That is a poor sword," he said. "And too big for you. Why don't you get something better, like this?" He swept out an elegant basket-hilted rapier. I raised my sword, ready for his attack.

Jacob jabbed the blade at me and I clumsily blocked it and stepped aside. Wallace's sword was much too heavy, and was made for a very different style of fighting. He came at me again, and I barely avoided being speared. I tried offensive, but he easily deflected my sword and jabbed at me again.

My life literally flashed before my eyes. I just had enough time to lean to the side before Jacob's sword ripped through my right shoulder, making a deep gash. At that point, I did the worst thing I could possibly do. I looked at it.

The blade had taken a large piece of my shirt with it, so I could easily see the gaping wound. I thought I saw a bone somewhere in there, too. Things started to turn reddish, and I lost all sense of where I was. Then searing pain came, and I felt like I was exploding. The right side of my shirt and pants were slowly soaking in blood. Something came in front of me like a reddish blur, and I lost consciousness.

Well, not quite.

I couldn't see where I was, and I could only hear one thing. Those annoying voices again, screaming at me:

The lost one will no more be lost

The boy will pay a heavy cost.

The boy will pay a heavy cost.

You will pay a heavy cost.

I haven't paid it already? I thought.

No. Just you wait.

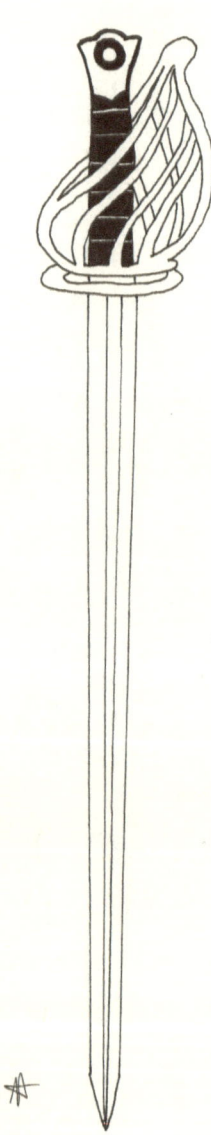

70

9. WE SCALE A CLIFF

The Nightmare. Again.

There we were again, James and I. I turned to look behind me and saw the thing moving along the hill. This time, I didn't go towards it. A pair of binoculars was in my hands, and I raised them to my eyes.

I focused in on that point, suddenly realizing it was a human shape, not an animal. I zoomed closer, and beheld the face of my cousin, Jacob, with a horrible grin of rage and satisfaction spreading across his face.

Suddenly, it all made sense. James's death was no accident! Jacob was responsible, and I knew why he had killed James. Both James and Jacob were my cousins, sons of my father's two older brothers. James's father was the oldest, and Jacob's mother the middle sibling, who had married John Mentieth. My father was Henry, the youngest son.

My grandfather, owned a lot of property. When he died, James was to inherit the main estate, as the only child of the oldest son. As a result, Jacob had always been jealous of this and had never liked James. Anyway, he was older than us, and never had more to do with us than he could help.

It hit me that Jacob, finally consumed by the greed that he had allowed to infiltrate him, and had murdered James in his eagerness to get the money he wanted. I finally realized what money did to people. It made them do things that they would otherwise not do, even to the point of murder.

*

When I woke up, I felt like I was on fire. My right shoulder was hurting so much I couldn't think straight. It took all my willpower to not scream. I tried to open my eyes fully and saw the vague shapes of people around me. Then I felt rocking and realized I was on a boat.

Someone touched my arm and I started, looking for who it was. I found myself staring at Mr. Stuart.

"Mr. Stuart!" I gasped. "Where are we? What's going on?"

"Hush," he calmed me. "We're goin' tae the Cinerean navy ship. We'll escape soon, and the mission will be over."

Over, I thought. *Over. Then I can go back to normal.* Then a sudden realization came to me. *But the Quest failed. Even if I finish it, I can never go back. I'm hunted now. I can never be me again. I can't go back to my old home. Where will I go?*

I turned my head to look at my shoulder, and it had been neatly bandaged up, probably by Mr. Stuart. My head pounded, and I realized I was hungry. I hadn't eaten anything since we were in the jail, which was something like thirty-six hours ago.

"Want somethin' tae eat?" Offered Donald, who was sitting next to me, rowing the boat. He fished with one hand in a large bag at his side, coming up with a biscuit. "A little dry, but still tastes good," he said, handing it to me.

"Thanks," I said weakly, still in a lot of pain from my shoulder. "Glad to see you awake. I guess my first aid job wasn't so bad."

"Probably saved my life," replied Donald. "Though I guess it was mostly my fault, thinking I could just ignore a wound like that. Cinerean healing works magic, though. I feel great."

We rowed on and on under the shadows of the cliff. Mr. Stuart, Beau and Hill were whispering together.

"Ye cannae be serious," Mr. Stuart was saying.

"I tell you, this is where they were!" Replied Hill.

"They probably got sunk, or eaten by the Loch Ness Monster." Grumbled Beau.

"Beau, stop bein' like that!" Scolded Mr. Stuart. "It isnae helpful. And do ye ken naething about Scottish geography? Loch Ness is nowhere near here, and it's an inland lake. Besides that, the Loch Ness Monster was a fake."

"I personally think that the most likely thing would be that they were driven off by the English Navy," commented Hill. "Otherwise, I don't know what would have happened."

"What happened?" I asked. "Who's gone?"

"Be quiet and rest, Kenneth," said Hill. "You don't need to worry about that."

"You don't need to protect me," I said, "I'd really like to know what's happened."

"Well," conceded Mr. Stuart, "The Cinerean ship is gone, and we donnae ken what tae do about it."

*

Night fell, cloudy and black. Scottie, who almost miraculously had made it through all our troubles, was in the boat with me. We found a little beach and dragged the boats onto it. Well, Beau, Hill, Donald, Mr. Stuart, and the other men did. They wouldn't let me help because of my shoulder. Not like I would have been much help anyway.

Hill and Mr. Stuart paced around, arguing in whispers over what to do. Beau grumbled silently to himself, sitting in the shadows under the cliff wall. I was too tired to do much of anything, so Donald and I talked together about what had happened to us.

Suddenly, Donald went quiet in mid-sentence. I looked at him in surprise. He was staring past me, and I turned for a glimpse at what he saw. I didn't see much, just two little points of light.

"What is it?" I asked in a whisper.

"People," he replied. "English, probably. Scouts. I cannae see clearly."

Beau's men slunk silently away as Hill and Mr. Stuart returned.

"Scouts," they whispered. "We sent Beau and his men to waylay them as quick as possible."

"What do we do?" Asked Donald.

"Stay here with Kenneth. Beau and his men are experienced and can easily master their own number in English troops."

At that moment, shadowy shapes began creeping out from behind rocks about fifteen yards away.

"What's that?" I asked.

Nobody replied. I was terrified. Beau was gone, and there was no way I would be able to use Wallace's sword with only one hand. We jumped up and began edging our way towards the cliff. Donald put Scottie in his backpack. Hill found a passable way along the side, and we began climbing up it, not wanting to be trapped between the sea, soldiers, and a sheer cliff. I made my way up as well as I could, using only my left arm to pull myself along. It was tough going, and I heard them —whoever they were—ascending up behind us.

Donald, still in the front, hauled me up onto a short ledge. I looked up, and saw we had at least halfway to go before we reached the top, and our pursuers were fast gaining on us. Also, there was no guarantee that there weren't fifty others waiting for us at the top. At any rate, the plateau above us would be better ground for fighting on than rocky sand.

The pursuers were nearly upon us now. I was exhausted, and my shoulder began to ache again. Hill, at the rear, drew his sword and began using it to pull himself up. Donald helped me up onto another small ledge, and we kept going. I slipped multiple times and would have fallen without him.

Our pursuers caught up to us, but didn't try to pull us down. Either they were so tired that they couldn't, or they were waiting to capture us on the cliff. The second idea was more likely.

At last, Donald reached the top, grabbed my left hand, and pulled me up. The ground was rocky and hard. I lay on the top, gasping for breath. Donald pulled up Hill and Mr. Stuart, and drew his sword. I picked myself up.

"Donald, go!" Mr. Stuart yelled. "Take Kenneth wi' ye!"

"Not without you!" I said. I grabbed his arm to try and pull him away. Hill shoved us all forward, and we began to run to the shelter of some rocks. Suddenly, there was a gunshot, and we threw ourselves down.

In the light of the waning moon I saw the glint of a pistol as it was drawn. I didn't have time to yell or do anything before another shot sounded. Hill fell forward, tumbling off the edge of the cliff. Nobody had any time to react before there was another shot, and Mr. Stuart fell backwards onto the ground. Answering shots rang out from behind us, and Donald pulled me down. Beau and his men had arrived.

Our pursuers attempted to flee back down the cliff, and Beau didn't try to stop them. It would have been too dangerous. Donald was by his father, with another Cinerean that looked like a doctor. Some others were by Hill. I came over, hoping that they were still alive. One look at Hill crushed my hopes. He had been shot in the head, and they were already wrapping him up in blankets. Mr. Stuart was unconscious, but still breathing. They began carrying them over to where the ship was, about a mile down the coast. I followed.

*

They put Mr. Stuart in a little cabin on the flagship. The doctor looked grave, and Beau was gloomier than I had ever seen him. Donald sat in a chair by the bed, staring blankly. Mr. Stuart opened his eyes and looked at us.

"Donald," he said, hoarsely. Donald looked up. "Give my sword to Elise, and tell her to take my place," he said. "The children of the Stuart Kings must live on."

I didn't understand what he meant. The Stuarts were once the kings of England and Scotland until the usurpation of William and Mary, but I didn't know Prince Charles had had any children.

Mr. Stuart slowly reached to the bedside table and grasped the blade of his sword. He turned the hilt towards Donald. Donald lifted it, but kept it in the sheath.

"It was Prince Charles's sword," Mr. Stuart said, weakly, turning to me. "I am descended from him." Donald absently handed the sword to me, as Mr. Stuart surveyed the cabin around us in surprise.

"Where's the Stone?"

He never spoke again.

10. DEATH IS IMMINENT

"We've got to face it," said Beau, burying the point of his pocketknife in the table. "We are all going to die."

I stared out the cabin window onto the cold, churning sea. "You certainly are not boosting my hopes."

"I wasn't trying to. I didn't know you had any hope left."

I rolled my eyes and plunged my hands into my hair. Mr. Stuart and Hill were both dead, and what I needed was some encouragement. I guess I shouldn't have expected it because however hard you tried, you would never get any kind of encouragement from Beau. Or anybody on the ship for that matter. Donald was out of action, and the only creature that really seemed to care about me was Scottie.

Scottie had miraculously come out of everything we had been through. After I had lost the Stone, Scottie had followed the men that took Donald and was eventually got found by Beau outside the jail. He was safe (for now) aboard the ship with us. It was as if he were magic.

Most of the time, Scottie stuck by Donald, except when he was hungry. Then he would come to me. Poor Donald! I pitied him. He was just sitting in the corner by the bed where his father was, and wouldn't pay any attention to anything going on around him. Elise was gone too—she was in Cinerea, and certainly knew nothing about her father's death.

I pondered everything that had happened, trying to think of some genius plan. But nothing came. Beau kept on stabbing the table with his knife, making a hard *thonk* every time he did it.

"So Mr. Stuart's descended from Charles Stuart?" I asked Beau.

"Yep."

"So why doesn't Donald wear the sword, and why did Mr. Stuart say to give it to Elise?"

Beau snapped his knife shut. "Because Elise is Malcolm's only child. Donald's adopted."

Wanting to know what was going on in the wide world outside the ship, I went to the desk and pulled out Elise's miniature radio. I had to rack my memory for a while to remember the frequency that Jacob used. I finally got it tuned and sat down to listen.

Hey Boss?

Who's this?

Rock and roll.

Good. What have you got to report?

We're up at 2pm tomorrow.

And?

The rock's gonna roll. We picked out a nice volcano for it, Boss.

Haha! Good! Tell you what. While you're off on your business, I'm gonna go to Cinerea myself. I got their precious Stone, why not rub it in their faces? Maybe I'll blow up the whole island while I'm at it.

But they have magic borders, Boss.

They do not! I'll prove it to you. And you'll see for yourself.

OK, Boss. Hope you're right.

I am and you know it. Over and out.

I switched off the radio and stared out the window, trying to pierce through the gloomy haze, I heard a sound besides the sound of Beau's knife. Wanting a change of scenery, I ran up onto the deck to investigate. I certainly saw something unexpected, but it was not a good surprise.

It was so foggy, nothing could be made out clearly. I couldn't see where the ship ended, just darker spots of mist. There were shouts all around, but I couldn't tell where they were coming from. Then the fog began to clear.

I looked to my right and I looked to my left. To both sides were a fleet of navy ships. One was large and one was small. One bore the Scottish flag, and the other the English. I was literally in the middle of a full-on naval battle. Just then, a round of machine gun bullets whizzed close by me. The great English-Scottish naval combat had begun.

Not wanting to get shot, I bolted for the stairs and rushed below deck, along with several of the men on guard up there. Bursting into the cabin, I yelled for all I was worth, "Beau! We've got to get out of here!"

"Why?" Asked Beau, finally laying his knife down on the heavily scored table. "What do we need to move for?"

"Well," I began, "We're right in the middle of a big naval battle. This ship's made of wood, and we need to get out of here before we're sunk—literally."

"We're all going to die, just like my father and Malcolm. They've got the Stone. We can move, but we can't save the Stone."

"*Beau!*" I screamed. "Get out of your mood! I know you've never been the most optimistic person, but at least do something! There might be some way we can save it! Command your men, or I'll do it for you!"

"Kenneth," said Beau, standing up, "I tell you, there is nothing. *Nothing*. We've failed and three of our friends are dead. That's half of us. Donald is too upset to help, and no blame to him. I can't do more, and you can't either."

"But there has to be something!" I said desperately. I needed to find a way, but I felt like I must accept Beau's advice: that there was not. Beau gave the order that we were to sail out of the bay, but I still had no idea what was going to happen. I watched the advanced warships pressing forward, coming closer to our wooden ship, tiny compared to England's great battleships.

"Where are we going?" I asked nobody in particular.

"To Cinerea," someone said. "There's nothing for us here."

I felt horrible, but I thought that they were right. I had gotten Mr. Stuart and Hillel killed, and the Stone was gone. Jacob was right, too. The day was his. I decided to go to bed and try to sleep it off. Donald wasn't in the cabin we shared, so I supposed he still hadn't left Mr. Stuart.

When I woke up, water was filling my cabin. I didn't have time to think about why because I needed to concentrate on how to get out. I grabbed Wallace's sword and buckled it on, the water reaching to my knees.

The water was seeping in from under the door, and I knew that if I opened it, the force of the water coming in would instantly fill the cabin and prevent my escape. My only hope was the window.

Pulling out the sword, I swung it as accurately as I could toward the window. I missed by a yard. It was high above me, and difficult to reach. I tried it again, but hit short of the mark. The sword was too heavy.

I picked it up with both hands, and gradually raised the point against the wall, the waterline creeping higher all the while. I succeeded in getting the tip up to the edge of the window and pushed as hard as I could. The point went through the glass, shattering it. I shoved the sword up, and it split through the middle.

The next difficulty was how to get up. I tied the strap of the back sheath to my wrist, and drove the point of Wallace's sword into the floorboards. Grabbing Prince Charles's sword from on top of the dresser, I belted it on and stood on the hilt of Wallace's sword, and pulled myself up to the window ledge, careful of broken glass. I got some in my hands anyway.

Tugging the sword point out of the floor and sheathing it, I flopped out, the swords hanging from me.

I hit the water with a huge splash, and had difficulty getting myself back to the surface. The ship slowly broke apart behind me. I grabbed onto a wooden beam and hauled myself onto it. Slowly I began to propel it toward the shore, which was not very far, but not very close either.

*

I sheltered from the rain behind a rock and tried to make a mental list of what to do. It looked something like this:

1. Don't die.

2. Save the Stone.

3. See if my friends are alive.

4. Find Jacob.

5. Destroy Jacob.

6. Figure out what you heard on the radio.

Item six seemed like the only thing I would be able to do at this point, so I pondered what I had heard on the radio.

Up at 2 pm.

The rock's gonna roll.

Maybe they were moving the Stone at 2 pm? Obviously, that what was meant by 'rock'. I also thought about 'the rock's gonna roll'. Referring to its destruction? Also, they had said they had picked out a nice volcano for it. To drop it into! If that was true, I had less than twenty-four hours to save the Stone before they took it for destruction.

Mentally checking off Item six, I looked around me in an attempt to fulfill Item three. As I suspected, I didn't see anyone, neither friend nor foe.

Looks like I'm doing okay on Item one, I thought. *It looks like two, four, and five are all going to have to happen at once, if at all.*

I stood up and decided that I was going to try and find Jacob, no matter what. About three seconds after that, I concluded that that was more easily said than done because I had just realized that I had zero idea where Jacob and the Stone was right now. I decided to go back to Item three and find someone who had a better idea than I did.

But who? There was nobody left to help me. I was on my own. Jacob was going to Cinerea, and I made up my mind to follow him, even if I had to do it all alone. I would do it for Mr. Dunnigan, for Hill, for Mr. Stuart, and for Donald, Beau, and Scottie, who probably were dead too.

11. The Traitor's Bane

I waded into the water until it reached my knees, trying to figure out which way Cinerea was. I wondered if Herbert or one of his turtles was around. All of a sudden, I was jerked off my feet and I hit my face on something hard. That something was moving at an incredible speed out onto the ocean. I grabbed onto it, looking wildly about to see what it was.

My head was out of the water, but my arms were wrapped around a scaly-feeling object that was taking me out to sea at over sixty kilometers an hour.

"*Herbert!*" I yelled, relieved. "You came in the nick of time, friend."

"Looks like it." The magic turtle replied. "Y'all were taking absolutely *forever* to get back, so Elise sent me to find everyone. What's funny is I was told there were five of you. The names were Beau, Hill, (two very old friends of mine), Malcolm and Donald (met them a couple of times), and Kenneth (which is you, right?). So anyway, I haven't seen any more of you. Can you tell me where the rest are so I can send the squad to go get them?"

"I'm Kenneth, you're right," I replied. "As for the others, both Mr. Stuart and Hillel are dead, and Beau and Donald might be too, for all I know."

"That's bad," observed Herbert. "Besides them being wonderful people and all, Malcolm had this sword (sword of Prince Charles, I'm told), and if he's dead, the sword is lost. There's prophesies about that sword, you know."

"Well," I said, "I didn't know there were any prophesies, but I've got it."

"There are prophesies galore! The main one is usually said in poetic form, but I'll abbreviate it here. Basically, there was a sword that belonged to Prince Charles—I'm sure you know who Prince Charles is, right?"

"Actually," I admitted, "I don't."

"Really!" exclaimed Herbert. "Well, basically all you really need to know is that the Stuarts were once kings of both England and Scotland. In around the mid- 1600s (I think) they got usurped by this guy named William and had to go into exile in France. Well, time went on and the heir to the throne was this kid named Prince Charles. He goes to Scotland and raises a rebellion, but it gets defeated, and he flees to France. Nobody knows, but he was secretly married and had a son, who had kids, and so on, until Malcolm was Charles's heir and got his sword. Clear?"

I nodded.

"Okay, so the main prophecy is that Charles's sword is going to get passed down to someone, and that someone will be the parent of the true King. The true King will eventually find the sword and come back to Scotland to raise the third rebellion against England and free Scotland. Understand?"

"Think so," I said. "Quite a lot to chew on."

"I know it's rather vague, but most prophesies usually are."

"Yes," I agreed, slowly. I was still thinking about the sword and why it had come to me. Was I the 'right' person? Had the sword come to me for a reason? But it was Elise's sword, so if I got to Cinerea, I would have to give it to her.

"Where are you taking me, Herbert?" I asked.

"To Cinerea. That's where you wanted to go, right?"

"Yes, but—"

"No time for that, pal. We gotta go fast. Hold on!"

*

"See that?" Asked Herbert, as we sped along.

"Sorry," I said. "I don't." My mouth was dry. I was probably sunburned, and hoped that we didn't have much longer to go.

"Well, it's the coast of Cinerea," Herbert continued. "We'll be there in about an hour."

"And what's the plan when we do get there?" I asked, relieved.

"Well, from what you've told me, Jacob might already be there by now. If you defeat him, maybe you'll get information on where the Stone is."

"I thought your magic borders would destroy him."

"He's smart. He won't get close enough for that."

I tried to think, but in my present situation it was difficult. Going to Cinerea, dueling Jacob, and getting the Stone, sounded easy enough, but I knew that putting the plan into action would need a lot more consideration.

*

"Is this the place?" I whispered to Herbert.

"Yes. I'm honestly surprised he got this far without getting destroyed. Anyway, I can't help you anymore from here. Good luck!"

"Thanks for everything!" I said, as Herbert disappeared into the water.

"You're welcome, pal. See you around!"

Making sure that both swords were securely belted to me, I grabbed onto the railing and hauled myself to the deck of the yacht. It was obviously Jacob's, a top-of-the-line pleasure ship with every modern convenience you could possibly stick in a boat. It was early morning, and nobody was out on deck. Mustering all the courage I had left (which wasn't a lot, let me tell you) I drew William Wallace's sword and yelled as loud as I could:

"Jacob, I'm here! I know you killed James!"

Jacob emerged from the cabin, sword drawn, and sneering.

"Wow! Never thought you'd be this brave. Are you in your right mind?"

"Yes, I am completely sane. I know you killed James so that you could get all his money when his father died. You murdered your own cousin!"

For a brief moment, I had a hope that Jacob would back down. I had a hope that when his dastardly scheme was revealed, he would admit defeat. Give me back the Stone. Retire in obscurity. Much to my dismay, he gave me a look of blank surprise.

"Was that supposed to bother me?"

I was horrified. He murdered his own cousin, and it didn't even faze him! Not having a reply to his question, I asked one myself.

"Where's the Stone? I've come for it. You had better tell me now."

"Tell you? Why, may I ask? Or haven't you realized that I've won?" Sneered Jacob.

"You haven't won yet," I replied. "Come on!" I raised the sword. "Try me!"

"They say third time's the charm, Walter," said Jacob. "But I think that it will be an unlucky charm for you." Suddenly, like lighting his sword flashed, and mine rang and shook my right hand so that I couldn't use it for a couple of seconds. I instinctively threw my left hand up in front of my face to protect myself as his sword shone again, and it came down on my left hand, cutting it completely off.

Through the blackness that began to overtake me, I had just enough brains left to lift the sword, point first at Jacob, even as he hewed at me once more for what he thought would be the finishing stroke. As he came forward, I did too, and I slipped under his blow.

My aim was true, and Jacob, who had unwisely left his chest unprotected as he raised his sword for one more slash, was speared through the heart by William

Wallace's sword. I fell onto the deck, him under me, and he never got up.

12. THE ADVENTURE ENDS—FOR NOW

My senses still spinning, I looked around in the water for the familiar multicolored glow of Herbert. I couldn't really tell whether I saw him or not because my eyes weren't working correctly.

Remembering my mistake when I glanced at my shoulder wound earlier, I didn't look at where my hand used to be, but ripped a piece off of Jacob's jacket with my right hand and balled it on there. Feeling the ball of cloth getting wet with blood, I ripped off another strip and used my teeth and right hand to tie it as tightly as I could, hoping to cut off the blood flow, so I didn't bleed to death.

The relief I should have felt at the death of my arch-enemy hadn't hit me yet because though I had been able to knock out items four and five on my to-do list, I was still pre-occupied with item one: *don't die.*

"Herbert?" I called weakly. "Herbert?"

"Hey there, pal!" Came a voice from behind me. I turned around and saw Herbert, in the water. "Oof, you look terrible. Whatcha do to your hand?"

"I can't talk about that right now," I groaned, fighting against unconsciousness. "Look, I need to get back to Cinerea before I bleed to death."

"Here, get on me," said Herbert. "Climb down."

I attempted to, but only being able to use one hand, I slipped off the side and fell heavily onto Herbert.

"Oof! Watch it, pal! OK, let's go!"

We weren't far from Cinerea, and judging by Herbert's speed (which he claimed was 321 kph at tops) it took us about fifteen minutes. When we arrived, a couple of people on the docks took one look at me and loaded me in a cart to get rushed to the hospital. At least, I hoped it was going to be a hospital. I was unconscious before I got there.

*

When I woke up, I had no idea what day it was or how long I had been asleep. I was in an old-fashioned wooden bed in a small stone room with a wooden door. There were tapestries on the walls, and on the table next to my bed was a bowl with a pitcher of water in it.

What a horrible dream I had, I thought to myself. *Wonder where I am.*

Wait, said another part of me. *That wasn't a dream. That was real.*

But I don't want it to be real!

Well, let's find out.

I looked at where my hand should be, hoping I would find it there. However, I was disappointed. I saw only my arm down to a little above the wrist, and at the end, lots of bloodstained bandages.

Great. It wasn't a dream. So much for those hopes.

Then another thing hit me.

The Stone! Item two on your list! Where is it?

Jacob's dead, so it's saved...right?

Nope. They've probably dropped it into a volcano by now.

Just then, Beau and Donald, with Scottie trotting at their heels, walked in.

"Donald!" I yelled at the top of my lungs. *"You're alive!"*

"Scottie and I got rescued by Herbert's gang," he said with a smile. "How are ye?"

"Missing a hand, but besides that, I'm mostly fine. But our mission failed. I killed Jacob, but I couldn't save the Stone." Then I looked closer at Beau. For the first time since I had known him, Beau laughed.

"I've got some good news for you, then!" He said. "Let's start at the beginning. So, you know that Jacob was planning on having the Stone dropped in a volcano?" He continued, still grinning. "Well, in their hurry to destroy the Stone, they flew just a little too close to Cinerea on their way to the volcano. I think they were going to El Salvador or someplace obscure like that. Anyway, our magic messes with their navigation instruments, and directs their course right over Cinerea. So they flew over the island—and, well, they got eliminated."

"So then the Stone went down with them!" I cried in dismay.

"Yes, and no," said Beau. "Yes, the Stone went down with it, but no, it's not destroyed. They crash-landed on Cinerea. The pilot and crew were all killed, but the Stone was safe inside. We're here to take you to see it placed into the secret vault we've created for it."

"It's *what?*" I yelled. "Safe? Now I know why you're happy for once, Beau!"

Donald rolled a little chair on wheels from behind the door. They helped me get into it and pushed me out of my little room. Scottie followed behind us.

We walked through passages of stone, and inside doorways I caught glimpses of candlelit halls and banquet chambers. When we came out into a courtyard, I caught my breath when I saw the massive towers and gates. The door wards pulled them open, and we stood on the edge of a perfectly shaped hill, with a road winding down, disappearing into the trees below. We faced North, and North, East, and South, I saw where two rivers met.

"To the North," said Beau, "you see where Ursa Forest meets the Seal Beach, and beyond them is Tropical Bay. Look West and you'll see the Turtle River. The Seal Beach is on its north bank, and the Cervus Mountains on its South. This castle is Falconhurst, home of the King of Cinerea."

The woods were so green, and the beaches so perfect, and the mountains so purple, I could well believe that this was a magic island.

"You live here?" I asked Beau.

"Yes, I do," he replied.

"You must be one of the luckiest men on earth."

"Not exactly a man," replied Beau.

"What?" Then I looked closer. He had taken his cap off. "Your ears are *pointed?*" I exclaimed. "You're a fairy?"

Beau grimaced. "Please, when you're around us, do NOT EVER say the word 'fairy', 'fay', 'little folk', 'brownie', or any other such unfortunate word. Your word 'fairy' has grown out of a wrong and diminutive interpretation of who we really are. The reason the mis-interpretation exists is because our enemies, when we fled to this land, wanted everybody to forget what we could actually do (namely totally annihilating them) and reduce us to a myth."

"You fled?" I asked. "Why did you flee if you could just destroy all your enemies?"

"Long story," said Beau. "We had two options. Wipe everyone off of the face of the earth (innocent or other-wise), or leave and establish a refuge our enemies would never find. We chose the latter, sailed West (be-fore any of you humans even knew that the Americas existed) and combined our failing power into one gem, which now sustains our magical borders. There's a lot of power in that gem. A reckless power, some have called it, and they're not wrong. Wisdom, however, bids us save it and not use it irresponsibly. Actually, we had another option, but my people can be really stubborn sometimes. Let's not talk about that."

"So I can't call you a—well, the word you told me not to say, so what can I call your people?"

"Well," began Beau, "The word in our tongue isn't really translated in any modern languages, but I guess the closest translation might be 'wise ones.' But it doesn't matter to you anyway. You can just call us Cinereans. That's who we are now."

We came to the edge of the Turtle River, and there Herbert and his gang pulled us downriver on a small ferry that was as sparkling and glittery as Herbert's shell. As they paddled, Herbert introduced his gang to us.

"The green one's George," he said, "my personal assistant. To the left there's Bob Blue, and Roger Red. There's also Orlando Orange, Perry Purple, and York Yardley Yellow. We call him 'Yada' because he talks to much and—"

"Yada, yada, yada," interrupted York. "They say my name's too long, and that I interrupt way too often. Herbert can spend ten million years complaining about me and not finish."

"I can well believe that," I replied.

*

Eventually, we came to where the Turtle River met the Bob River, (yes, named after Bob Blue) and we took its road down to the sea. As we passed by another river's mouth, Orlando called,
"That's the mouth of the Orlando, named after me!"

"Yes," replied Yada, "and there's a Herbert and a Perry, and a Roger, and a George, and a Yada too."

We went close to the coast, sailing in the Stingray Bay near the Lotar Forest, until we came to the end of the western peninsula. Fort Kay stood there, towering above the trees on a hill of stone.

"That's our destination," announced Roger. "Hope ya like it!"

We landed on the shore, and Beau and Donald rolled my chair to the foot of the hill. Many Cinereans stood there, all with black hair and sea-grey eyes. One came up and talked with Beau excitedly in some strange fairy language. Elise was with them, wearing Prince Charles' sword, and she joined us. The other people stood in a nearly full circle around the Stone of Destiny, on a type of flat cart with wheels and no sides.

The Cinereans sang a slow song in a strange language. Silver lines began to appear on the door, and they formed a doorway. Slowly, the rock moved aside, and the Stone of Destiny was sealed.

Then, I noticed two long boxes nearby, shaped a little like coffins. Beside it was a smaller box. The people picked them up and put them on either side.

"What are those?" I asked.

"Those are the bodies of Hillel and my father," Elise answered. "The small box is in memory of Chester Dunnigan. We were unable to retrieve his body."

Suddenly, the sorrow of what had happened on that cliff came back to me. But in the midst of it was joy, that Mr. Stuart and Hill could be buried next to the Stone they gave their lives to save.

Then I heard Beau speak.

"James," he said. "Come out."

James? What does he mean by James? He can't mean my cousin.

Beau looked down at Scottie, and so I did too. Right before my eyes, Scottie began to grow. The Sword, held by Elise began to shine too, and eventually, I had to shut my eyes, so great was the light it gave out.

As the light dimmed, I opened my eyes. Standing before me, was a boy about my own age, with a huge smile on his face.

"Hey, Walter!" He said. "Long time no see!"

"James?" I said in disbelief. "It can't be you. You fell off the cliff!"

"Fairy magic can be a little unpredictable," said Beau. "There was a Cinerean with Herbert at that time, who was unfortunately a novice at casting spells. Instead of slowing James's fall, she accidentally turned him into a dog, and made the spell irrevocable until his would-be assassin was killed. I assure you she was soundly lectured on her mistake." He said, looking at the Cinerean who had spoken to him a little while before. She laughed nervously.

The words of the prophecy came back to me.

The lost one will no more be lost
That boy will pay a heavy cost.

Finally, the prophecy was fulfilled. I felt nearly completed, but something was still bothering me. I didn't know what it was, so I simply said,

"Magic or no, it's amazing to see you back."

"Same. Are you going back to Scotland? Your true name, Walter Percy, is in honor there."

"I'm sorry; James, but I don't think so."

"Why not?"

"There's another prophecy, James, and it has to do with the Sword and the King."

"But Walter…"

"James, I'm so sorry, but I feel like I still have to do something. I won't leave now, in fact, I have no idea where I am going. For now, I'll live in Cinerea and recover. You can stay with me here, if you like."

"I suppose…I haven't got much to go back to. Thanks to Jacob, I'm presumed dead. They'd never believe me if I tried to go back. How long do you think you'll stay?

"A couple of years, maybe," I said. "I don't know where the Sword will take me, but I know I can't go into a new world at eighteen."

"Makes sense, Walter!" Agreed James. "I'll stay with ye. Maybe I'll go back to Scotland, we'll see."

"You made a good choice, Walter," said Beau, using my real name for the first time. "Wait here for a while. And then let the Sword take you where it will."

*

Three years later, I stood in the bedroom of our apartments in the castle of Falconhurst. I had married Elise in the great banqueting hall a year earlier, and our child had been born only a few hours ago. James and his wife, a Cinerean, were also there.

"What do you think his name should be?" I asked Elise.

She considered for a minute, and then spoke.

"Malcolm."

"It's time," said Beau, who stood behind me.

"Time?" I asked.

"Draw the Sword."

I drew the Sword out from where it always hung by my side. Elise grabbed my hand, and little Malcolm put his on the hilt. It began to shine, and its white light grew brighter by the second.

"Save the Sword for your son!" I heard Beau crying faintly, as if from far away. "Farewell! You're going to the land of the free, and the home of the brave. Prepare baby Malcolm for the day when he will fulfill the rest of the prophecy! Farewell!"

About the Author

If you benefited from this book, please consider posting an online review. Thank you in advance.

Alexandria Adair, a 17-year-old homeschooled senior, is an ardent enthusiast of all things Scottish. At the tender age of 12, she embarked on a history assignment that led her to uncover her Scottish heritage through her family tree, tracing it back to the illustrious Clan Maxwell. This discovery ignited a passion within her, prompting her to delve deeper into Scottish history. Her dedication resulted in the writing of two captivating novels: *The Stone of Destiny* and its sequel, *Reforged*. These novels transport readers to the past, recounting the stories of the Stuart clan and the Jacobites' fervent hope for the restoration of the true King.

In addition to her literary pursuits, Alexandria is also a professional bagpiper, showcasing her talent by competing solo and with her band.

Visit the author's website at
https://alexandriaadair.com/

Follow on social media:
Instagram: https://www.instagram.com/alexandri-a_e_adair

About the Publisher

Sulis International Press publishes select fiction and nonfiction in a variety of genres under four imprints:

- Riversong Books (fiction)

- Sulis Press (general nonfiction)

- Keledei Publications (spirituality)

- Sulis Academic Press (academic works)

For more, visit the website at
https://sulisinternational.com

Subscribe to the newsletter at
https://sulisinternational.com/subscribe/

Follow on social media
https://www.facebook.com/SulisInternational
https://twitter.com/Sulis_Intl
https://www.pinterest.com/Sulis_Intl/
https://www.instagram.com/sulis_international/